Nice Mice

Max and Maggie in
SUMMER

Written by Janet Craig

Illustrated by Paul Meisel

WHISTLESTOP ®

Troll Associates

For Stephen—
J.C.

Library of Congress Cataloging-in-Publication Data

Palazzo-Craig, Janet.
Max and Maggie in summer / written by Janet Craig;
illustrated by Paul Meisel.
p.   cm.—(Nice mice)
Summary: Two mice friends enjoy the pleasures of
summer—fishing, picnicking, and watching clouds.
ISBN 0-8167-3352-X (library) — ISBN 0-8167-3353-8 (pbk.)
[1. Mice—Fiction. 2. Summer—Fiction.
3. Friendship—Fiction.]   I. Meisel, Paul, ill. II. Title.
III. Series: Palazzo-Craig, Janet.   Nice mice.
PZ7.P1762Max 1994
[E]—dc20   94-6084

CONTENTS

SUMMER FUN

"It's summer!" said Maggie Mouse to Max Mouse. "What a special time of year this is!"

The two friends were sitting in the shade, sipping cold lemonade. "I think so, too," said Max. "I love the summer. It's warm and sunny."

"And you can play outside almost every day," added Maggie.

Max took another sip of lemonade. "What should we do today?" he asked.

"Something special," said Maggie. "Something special for a special day."

Maggie and Max thought for a minute. Then, at exactly the same moment, each one said, "I know!"

Maggie giggled. "You first," she said.

"I was going to say we could go on a picnic," said Max.

"Well, that might be nice," said Maggie. "But I was going to say we could go fishing."

"Fishing is fun," said Max. "But today is a great day for a picnic. We can pack a big lunch. And we can bring a ball to play with."

Maggie frowned. "I like picnics," she said. "But I think fishing is more fun."

"Well," said Max. "*I* want to go on a picnic."
"Well," said Maggie. "*I* want to go fishing."

"A picnic!" said Max.

"Fishing!" said Maggie.

The two friends glared at each other. Finally
Max said, "I am going on a picnic by myself.
You are going to miss a good time."

"That's what you think," said Maggie. "I'll be
too busy having fun fishing. And when I catch
a big fish, you'll be sorry!"

Then each mouse turned and stomped away.

Max got busy. He put a lot of good things to eat in a big picnic basket. He took a ball along, too. Then he set off for the pond to look for a good picnic place.

Meanwhile, Maggie gathered her fishing gear.
She carried everything to her favorite rock by
the pond.

Maggie started to fish. Across the pond,
she could see Max with his picnic basket.
"I wonder what Max brought to eat," she thought.
Maggie felt a little hungry—and a little lonely.

On the other side of the pond, Max watched
Maggie fishing. He opened his picnic basket.
Then he closed it. He did not feel very hungry.
"I wonder if Maggie has caught any fish,"
thought Max.

Max decided to go see Maggie. At the same
time, Maggie put down her fishing rod. She set
off through the woods to find Max.

It was not long before they met.

"Hi, Maggie," said Max, shyly.

"Hi, Max," said Maggie, just as shyly.
"How was the picnic?"

"Okay, I guess," said Max. "Catch any fish yet?"

"Not yet," said Maggie.

Max and Maggie were quiet. Then, at exactly the same moment, each one said, "I know!"

They laughed. "You first," said Max.

"I was going to say maybe we could have a picnic, and *then* go fishing," said Maggie.

"That's just what *I* was going to say," said Max.

So Max and Maggie ate. Then they played catch. Then they sat down on the rocks and fished.

"I love summer," said Max happily.

"Me, too," said Maggie. "There are so many fun things to do—especially when you have a friend to do them with."

"That's just what I was going to say!" said Max.

NOTHING TO DO

It was a beautiful day in the late part of summer, but Max Mouse was not happy.
"There's nothing to do," sighed Max.
"I'm so bored."

Lettuce

Max spun himself in a circle, hoping to think
of something to do. Max did not get any ideas.

What he *did* get was very dizzy.

"Phooey!" said Max. "I think I'll go see Maggie. Maybe she can think of something to do."

Max walked along. The sun was warm, but not too warm. Big, fluffy clouds moved across a bright blue sky. But Max did not notice any of those things.

When he came to his friend's house, Max called out, "Maggie, where are you?"

"Right here," said a voice. Maggie's head popped out of the tall garden grass. "What's wrong, Max?"

"I'm bored," he said. "There's nothing to do."

"You could read a book," suggested Maggie.

"I don't feel like reading," said Max.

"You could go for a ride on your bike," said Maggie.

"No," said Max, shaking his head.

"How about swimming?" said Maggie.

"I don't think so," said Max.

"Well," said Maggie, "you could do what I do when there's nothing to do."

"What?" asked Max.

"Come on," said Maggie. "I'll show you." She stretched out on her back in the grass. Then she put her hands behind her head for a pillow. Max did the same. The sun felt good on his face.

"Look at the clouds," said Maggie. "Aren't they pretty? There goes one that looks like a sailboat."

"And look at that one!" said Max. "Doesn't it look like a smiling face?"

The two mice saw clouds of all shapes and sizes pass across the sky.

"There goes a dragon," said Max.
"And a giant ice cream cone," said Maggie.
Max smiled. "I guess sometimes doing
nothing is better than doing something,"
he said.

And the two friends watched the summer
clouds until dark, when the first stars came out
to take their place.